WW WINGS

Anything is Possible When You Believe

That night, Vanessa told her parents that she was going to bed a little earlier than usual. She looked over her plan once again. She waited. She waited until she knew that everyone in the house was asleep. Vanessa's heart was pounding so hard; she was hoping that the sound of it wouldn't wake anyone up. She took the Internet addresses that Mrs. Techlander gave her and quietly left her room. She peeked her head into her parents' room to make sure they were both sound asleep. She continued to scamper like a mouse throughout the dark apartment and into the forbidden room. She followed her plan exactly as written. She entered the password: NoLimits. She was on her way to the Internet. She was working as quietly as she could, while exploring the sites that Mrs. Techlander had given her. But somehow, Vanessa wasn't too thrilled. The Internet was better than using the encyclopedias, but Vanessa realized she still had to generate a ten-page report somehow with all this information. The excitement had worn off. She had conquered doing something she wasn't supposed to. She looked at the clock. It was 2:00 a.m. She had to get up for school in a matter of hours. She shut down the computer and went to bed. She was disappointed that her late night Internet session hadn't been more adventurous.

When Vanessa went under the covers, she dreamed about having wings. Wings that could take her anywhere she wanted, whenever she wanted. If only she could have a pair of wings, she would be the happiest girl in the whole world.

WWW.WINGS

Anything is Possible When You Believe

M.A. Kokos Lambrou

Llumina Press

ISBN: 1-932047-16-6

Printed in the United States of America

*To my mother, Athanasia,
who fostered my creativity
and my ability to imagine.*

Author's Note

Although WWW.WINGS is a work of fiction, there are many messages that you, the reader can realize. I hope that you will read for enjoyment and walk away feeling content. In order to help you see some of the messages that I intended, I've included a special, brief section at the end of each chapter, *Something to think about.* Take a moment and read these as you read this book. On some pages, there may be an opportunity to write or draw. (Of course, if this book isn't your own personal copy, you may use another sheet of paper to write or draw.)

Enjoy the story. And remember, anything *is* possible, if you *believe.*

M.A. Kokos Lambrou

Chapter 1
The Snowstorm

She slammed her hand on the snooze button one more time, rolled over, and pulled the covers over her head in an effort to make herself invisible. Vanessa despised waking to the sound of the electrifying alarm clock, especially on a school day in the dead of winter. During the next ten minutes of "snooze sleep," she had visions of being someplace real warm.

She heard rhythmic sounds of ocean waves crashing against the shore. Sw-ish...sw-ish...sw-ish. She could see birds soaring in a cloudless sky, navigating in a precise v-shape. She could feel the sun's rays penetrating through her skin. It felt good. She was content.

Buzz-Buzz-Buzz--- SLAM! Vanessa put the annoying sound to a stop, disappointed to discover the warm thoughts were only an illusion. The clock read 7:20 a.m. She could not afford to sleep any longer. Vanessa forced herself to sit up. She positioned her legs over the edge of her bed, pushed off with her hands, and landed in her bunny slippers, awaiting her on the floor. Vanessa reached her arms way overhead, and stretched like a rubber band, as she let out a wide yawn. Vanessa put on her robe and shuffled her way into the living room. This was a usual part of her morning routine.

"Oh my goodness," Vanessa exclaimed, as she looked outside the living room window, "that dumb weather man *was* right on T.V. last night!"

Vanessa sat on the old-fashioned radiator in her family's apartment. Disappointment hung on her face as she gazed out at Brook Drive. Vanessa couldn't think of anything she hated more than the cold, winter snow; except of course, the piercing sound of an alarm clock. Most children loved snow, but to Vanessa it only meant the hassle of bulky jackets, boots, hats, scarves, mittens, turtlenecks, snow pants, and not to mention runny noses. Even though winter lasts only three months, they were the three most horrible months of the year. (Except of course, there was Christmas, which she loved, because she got lots of gifts.) Vanessa sat and stared out the window at the snow that fell so silently and sneakily while she was asleep.

Suddenly, she had a notion; maybe there would be no school today. Vanessa quickly jumped up from the radiator and ran to the kitchen where her mother was cooking breakfast.

"Mommy, did you see all of that snow outside?"

"Yes Nessa," her mother replied, "I already called your school and it *is* open. You need to sit down now and eat your breakfast."

Vanessa's demeanor changed in an instant. She slumped into her chair and began to eat.

Vanessa hated it when her mom knew just what she was thinking. How did her mom know that she was hoping for no school today? *Maybe my mom is psychic,* Vanessa thought. *She should go into business* *for herself and tell people their futures, just like those people on T.V. do. Those people on T.V. make like $3.00 per minute or something! Just think of what we could do with all that money!*

"Hey Mom," Vanessa said.

"Yes dear," replied her mom.

"I uh, um, oh, never mind."

Vanessa continued to eat her breakfast. She had a plan.

"Mom, could I please have more sausage, eggs, pancakes, and orange juice?"

"Don't you think you've already had enough?" Her mom asked as she squinted her eyes and shook her head.

"No, ma, I have a really big appetite this morning. It must be all that snow outside!" Vanessa said with a sly grin on her face.

Vanessa's mom gave her another glass of orange juice and said, "You need to finish eating so you can get yourself washed up for school."

Vanessa obeyed her mom and drank her orange juice. On the way to the bathroom, Vanessa ran into her brother's room and started to jump on his bed. Brandon was not awake yet. He had no choice but to awaken now.

"You are such a brat!" Brandon exclaimed, "Get off my bed and out of my room NOW!"

Brandon is older than Vanessa. He is in high school, and plays on the basketball team. He really thinks he is something special. Even though Vanessa always fights with Brandon, he is her only sibling, and she actually kind of admires him. She looks up to him. She hates it when he bosses her around.

With a pout on her face, she sunk her head and mumbled, " I was just trying to say good morning to you." Vanessa shuffled her feet as she grabbed her towel from the linen closet and went into the bath-room.

Vanessa took as much time as she possibly could in the bathroom. While she was in the shower, she washed her hair two times and she scrubbed her body with the washcloth for so long that her skin be-gan to turn red. She then brushed her teeth two times. As she put the toothpaste on the toothbrush to begin a third brushing, her mother knocked on the door.

"Vanessa, are you almost done in there? Bran-don needs to get ready for school, too."

"Yeah ma, I'm just about to brush my teeth," Vanessa replied.

In the meantime, Brandon had finished with his breakfast and he wanted to take his turn in the bath-room. He started pounding on the door so hard, Vanessa thought it was going to fall in on her.

"Hey!" Vanessa screamed, "You crazy or some-thing?"

Brandon didn't reply. He just kept pounding on the door.

"That's enough," Mother said in a firm voice.

Brandon stepped aside and allowed Mother to talk to Vanessa from outside the bathroom door, which was now locked.

"Vanessa Ashley Onero, I expect you to listen to me right this moment. Stop whatever you are doing, and come out of that bathroom now. And I mean NOW!" Mrs. Onero is the most caring and giving person you could know, but when you get her mad, you better watch out!

"Yes Mother, I am listening to you, but I have a bit of a problem," Vanessa said in her sweetest voice.

"What is it Vanessa? We don't have time for games. You need to get to school. The rest of us are running late now because of you!"

In her most sincere voice, Vanessa replied, "I have a really bad tummy ache."

Brandon walked away and muttered, "Not this again."

Mrs. Onero knew Vanessa's whole routine of the tummy ache. "Okay Vanessa, I'll get your things and take you to see Dr. O'Donohue before I go to the office."

No, not Dr. O'Donhue's office, Vanessa thought. She hated going to the doctor. If she wasn't already sick, she'd get sick after sitting in the doctor's office. She just hated how it smelled and how the doctor would ask her tons of personal questions.

"Okay Mom, I will be ready in a minute." Vanessa would rather spend a day traveling in the snow than visit Dr. O'Donohue! She quickly came out of the bathroom so Brandon could take his turn.

"Vanessa, you are such a brat! I am going to be late for school now! Just remember your little stunt. I'll pay you back, when you are least expecting it!"

Vanessa knew that her brother was angry, because at his school he received detentions for being late. Vanessa kind of felt bad, but she began to wonder what in the world he would do to get even with her.

Vanessa packed up her school bag and put on her winter attire. Mrs. Onero had already gone outside to start the car and clean off all the heavy snow. Vanessa tied her scarf tightly around her neck, and flung it over her shoulders as she headed for the brutal outdoors. The only thing Vanessa could think about on the way to school was how she could escape all the snow. *Maybe I could hibernate like bears do. It must be nice. They go to sleep and when they wake up, the weather is nice again.* Vanessa knew she was being ridiculous. On a more realistic note, Vanessa thought about how much she would love to live somewhere it was warm all year long, like Florida. *Oh my goodness, I could even get a season pass to Disney World!*

"Nessa, Nessa, VA-NES-SA!" Mrs. Onero was trying to get Vanessa's attention.

"Oh, yes Mom, I was uh...oh never mind."

"Exactly Vanessa, never mind and get out of the car. I'll be here to pick you up after school. I don't want any phone calls from the principal today, do you understand me?"

"Yes Mother," Vanessa replied. Vanessa got out of the car, disappointed that her daydream was interrupted. It was just getting good, too.

"Bye," Mom said with a smile.

Vanessa managed to say bye to her mom, even though she was mad at her. Vanessa tried to get back into her daydream as she walked through the deep snow towards the entrance of her school. Suddenly, Vanessa remembered something very important. She remembered when she took a family vacation to Florida. She was three. Her father said that someday he'd like to move there. This idea gave Vanessa some hope.

Vanessa walked to her locker. *Maybe this will be the last time I have to suffer with these bulky snow clothes.*

Vanessa walked into her classroom with a smile on her face. She had hopes of being in a warm climate real soon.

Something to think about......

The last name used for this family is "Onero." This word comes from the Greek language and it means "to dream." You will understand why I chose this name as you read on. Do you know words from other languages that could perhaps be used for character names?

Does Vanessa like the winter? How do you know?

Chapter 2
The Consequence

"Good morning Mrs. Techlander," Vanessa said with a smile.

"Well good morning Vanessa, I'm glad you could make it."

Vanessa looked around the room and noticed that she was the last to arrive. Instead of making up excuses, Vanessa quietly took her seat. Vanessa took out her social studies text and found her place. Joey, the boy who sits next to her, was shuffling around in his desk. Jeni was amusing herself by making faces at Erik. Mrs. Techlander was sitting on her stool in front of the class. Nothing was unusual.

The only thing Vanessa liked about the social studies book was the pictures. The class was studying regions of the United States. Vanessa was particularly interested in the Southeast. Florida is in the Southeast.

Mrs. Techlander was doing the boring routine of reading from the textbook. Vanessa got bored, as usual, and started to daydream. The last she could remember hearing was one of her classmates reading about the economy of Florida.

Why couldn't I be there, why? Vanessa's eyes were glued to the picture of a sunrise over the ocean. *God please, I'll do anything to live in a place that is al-*

ways warm. I promise God, that if you grant me this wish, I'll clean up my room everyday for the rest of my life. Plus, I'll never fake a tummy ache again, for as long as I live. And, because I want this so badly, I'll never do anything ever again to make Brandon late for school. So God, please help me. Vanessa thought about how the warm sun would feel, riding her bike to school in the morning. She could be free just to wear a t-shirt and shorts; no bulky clothes, gloves or any other winter attire she hated. *I bet all the children my age would always be happy in a state like Florida. It should be real easy to make new friends, since the kids probably play outside all the time. And just think of all the field trips the teachers could take us on to Walt Disney World.*

Vanessa was becoming so absorbed by her daydream, that she had forgotten where she was. Then Mrs. Techlander embarrassed her.

"Miss Onero, since you obviously are too intelligent to participate with us today, why don't you come up here and lead the class?"

Suddenly, the whole class was staring at Vanessa. Vanessa's face turned so red, and felt so hot, she thought her whole head was going to explode like a volcano! Mrs. Techlander sat down at her desk and waited for Vanessa to go up to the front of the room. This is not the first time that Vanessa was caught daydreaming. Mrs. Techlander really dislikes it when her students do not pay attention. Do it enough, and she'll embarrass you.

Vanessa went to the front of the class and said, "Florida is located in the Southeast. The capital is Disney World. I wish I could be there right now."

None of Vanessa's classmates said a word. The room was so silent; you could hear an ant moving. Mrs. Techlander did not yell and scream at Vanessa. She wasn't a yelling and screaming type of teacher. However, she did assign Vanessa extra work. Vanessa had one week to come up with a ten-page researched report on Florida!

Vanessa felt as if the whole roof of the building had just collapsed on her shoulders. She could not move. How could Mrs. Techlander do such a thing to her? She was only daydreaming a little. Big deal. Kids do that all the time. Who cares what the capital of Florida is anyway! Without a word, Vanessa sunk her head down and quickly took her seat.

"Now, would anyone else like to join Vanessa?" Mrs. Techlander asked with an attitude. All of the students were silent. You could hear the same ant moving.

"Okay boys and girls, let's get back to business." Vanessa was trying her hardest not to hate Mrs. Techlander. She put on her best pretending-like-she-was-paying-attention look.

That school day was the longest Vanessa had ever experienced in her life. It was so long, she could have walked from her school to Florida and back, and Mrs. Techlander would still be talking!

Something to think about......

Do you think what Mrs. Techlander did was fair? If you were the teacher, what would you have done?

Based on her personality, draw a picture of what you think Mrs. Techlander looks like. (You may use the space below, if this is your book).

Chapter 3
The Phone Call

When Vanessa's mom picked her up from school, Vanessa neglected to tell her about the social studies incident. Vanessa decided that she would just announce what happened with Mrs. Techlander at the dinner table that night. Maybe her father would feel guilty and take the whole family on a vacation to Florida. That way, Vanessa could write an excellent report for Mrs. Techlander. Until dinnertime came, Vanessa remained hopeful.

****

"Okay everyone, dinner is ready," Mrs. Onero called out.

Vanessa was the last one to arrive at the dinner table. She was trying to figure out how she could convince her family to go to Florida. Vanessa's mom made her favorite meal: chicken with roasted potatoes. Vanessa felt that dinner was off to a good start.

"So how was your day today Pops?" Vanessa asked cheerfully.

"Everyday is just about the same for me," Vanessa's father answered in a monotone.

"What about you Mom?"

"Oh, nothing special," Vanessa's mom said as she was cutting her chicken.

"Guess what," Brandon said.

"What," Vanessa replied.

"I've got a big secret, that I'm not gonna let you in on," Brandon said with a huge smile on his face.

Vanessa thought hard about what it could possibly be, but she really didn't care because she wanted to focus on her dad with this Florida thing.

"Anyway, does anyone want to know what happened to me today?" Vanessa asked.

"You mean besides your fake tummy ache that made me late for school," Brandon snapped.

Vanessa's father didn't have to say a word. He just gave her a hard stare. It was enough to make Vanessa feel guilty. Her father has ways of making his feelings known.

Just great. Brandon had to tell Dad what happened this morning. The last thing Vanessa needed right now was her father to be upset with her.

"So, as I was saying," Vanessa said calmly, while giving her brother a nasty glare, "Does anyone care to know what happened to me today?"

Vanessa's mom came to her aid, "Yes Nessa, I'd like to know. What happened to you today?"

Before Vanessa spoke, her heart did a few flip turns. "Well, in social studies, we are studying the regions of the United States. I have an assignment to write a report on Florida."

Vanessa looked at her father. He looked at his wife and said, "You know Vanessa, we could've been living in Florida right now, but your mother never wanted to go."

"Anyway," Vanessa continued, "I have to write a ten-page researched report, and it is due in a week."

"Oh my goodness," Mrs. Onero exclaimed. "That seems kind of lengthy for a fourth grade report. I didn't have to write a report that long until I entered college!"

"Well Mom, you know how Mrs. Techlander can be. She says that we don't learn anything unless we work hard. It's actually weird, but I can see her point."

"Well that's great to hear," Mr. Onero said with a smile on his face. "I'm not quite so sure that you are telling us everything. What's the catch?"

"Oh Dad, you always think that I am up to something. Maybe I'm just starting to really appreciate the good school I go to, that's all."

"Well, if that *is* all, I'm very pleased," Mrs. Onero said with a strange look on her face. She had no idea where Vanessa's appreciation for school was coming from, but as a parent, she really had no complaints.

Just then, the phone rang. Mrs. Onero didn't appreciate phone calls during dinner. She got up and went down the hall to answer the phone.

Perfect, Vanessa thought, *now I can butter up my dad into the whole Florida thing without my mom here.*

"You know Dad, I am actually kind of excited about my report on Florida. I do have good memories from the vacation we went on as a family. Didn't you always say that you would like to live there someday?"

15

"Yes, Vanessa, but you know how your mother is, she'll never leave the rest of her family here in Chicago," Dad said with an unhappy look on his face.

"I know Dad. We have lived here for all my life. Don't you think it is time for a change?"

"Vanessa, what are you trying to get at?"

"Well, I think I could write a fabulous report if I have first hand knowledge. I mean, I could look at pictures in the encyclopedia and all, but that really doesn't give me the whole effect. If I am actually there, I could *feel* how hot it is. I could *hear* how the ocean waves sound. I could *see* what the surroundings look like down there."

"Vanessa, I can see your point, but we all can't just pick up and go to Florida because you have to write a report on it. You'll just have to do what the other kids are doing, and use your books."

"Oh, Dad, but PLEASE, we could all use a vacation about now anyway. Did you see all that snow outside? It's awful. I know you don't like it either. PLEASE Daddy, please," Vanessa was starting to beg.

Before Mr. Onero could say another word, Mrs. Onero marched back into the kitchen with an unhappy, stern look on her face. "Brandon, please excuse yourself from the table. Your father and I need to talk to Vanessa."

"No problem Mom." Brandon got up from the table and went into his room.

Vanessa could smell trouble in the air, but she couldn't possibly figure out what her mother could be so mad about.

"Vanessa, that was Mrs. Techlander on the phone. It seems that you had a little trouble in class today."

Vanessa was silent. She was trying to think how she was going to wiggle her way out of this one. "Well you see Mom, it's not really what you think."

"Oh, no? Vanessa, don't even think about trying to get yourself out of this. You've caused enough trouble in one day. I want you to clean up this table and wash the dishes. When you are done, you may go to your room and stay there until your father and I come and talk to you about your punishment. Do you understand me?"

"Yes Mother."

Mr. Onero in the meantime had no idea what the problem was. "Honey, can I ask what she has done now?"

"Well, apparently, Vanessa has been giving zero effort in class. Today she was caught daydreaming. Furthermore, this assignment that Vanessa has to do was assigned to her because she hasn't been participating enough. Not everyone has to write a ten-page researched report."

As Vanessa was washing the dishes, tears welled up in her eyes. Her parents just didn't understand what it was like to be somewhere you didn't want to be. They also didn't understand how much she hated winter. If only they could move out of Chicago, all of her problems would be solved.

Mr. Onero was annoyed, "Vanessa, I can't believe that you were trying to convince me to take a vacation to Florida so you could write a report! You were

17

given the assignment in the first place as a punishment, and now you want to be rewarded with a vacation? You have a lot of nerve young lady!"

Vanessa let the tears roll down her cheeks as she finished washing the dishes. All she could think about now was what her next punishment would be. Vanessa shut off the water, dried her hands and went to her room.

Vanessa sat on her bed and stared out the window at the snow that refused to stop falling. She thought about her horrible day. First the snow had to come. Then she made her brother late for school. He said he was going to get even with her, and Vanessa couldn't imagine what he would possibly do to her. Then when Vanessa got to school, her teacher gave her a ridiculously long report to do. Now, both of her parents are mad at her. *I just don't get it. I'm not a bad child, why am I being treated like one?* Vanessa miserably sat in her room until her parents decided to grace her with their presence.

Something to think about......

Vanessa may have a case of the "winter blues." What do you do to fight the "winter blues" or boredom? Make a list of your favorites below.

Chapter 4
Good News Follows Punishment

Vanessa's mother and father entered her room like army sergeants. Vanessa's dad spoke first. "Well young lady, you made some bad choices today. You will have to accept the consequences. Your mother and I decided on a few new rules for you. First, every-day after school, you will come directly home and work on your homework. Second, your mother has added a few more chores to your list. Last, but not least, you are not allowed in my home office. I just had a new computer system installed and it is absolutely off limits for you! Now Vanessa, do I make myself clear?"

Vanessa felt too scared to answer her father.

"Don't just stare at me Vanessa, answer my question!"

Vanessa swallowed the lump she had in her throat and managed to say, "Yes Dad, I understand the rules."

Mr. Onero gave Vanessa a stern look right into her eyes just before he turned around and left the room. Mrs. Onero could see that Vanessa was quite upset. "Vanessa, your father and I think these new rules will help you. We don't understand why you are slacking off in school so much. Is there something bothering you that you'd like to talk to me about?"

"No Mom, it's not anything you can help me with," Vanessa mumbled, not even picking up her head to look at her mother.

Mrs. Onero lifted up Vanessa's chin so she could see her face. "What did you say under there?"

"I said, it's not anything you can help me with, unless you'd like to move to Florida," Vanessa snapped.

"Ooooh, so that's what all this is about. Vanessa, I don't understand why you dislike the winter so much. Most children your age enjoy playing in the snow; having snowball fights, making snow angels, building forts, and creating snowmen. If you keep using the snow and winter as an excuse for your behavior, you are going to have some serious consequences."

Vanessa could tell her mom just didn't understand. "Okay Mom, you've given me my punishment, and now you are trying to tell me I'm not normal because I don't like to play in the snow, like other kids my age. I need to be alone now."

Mrs. Onero did not want to upset Vanessa, so she simply turned around and left Vanessa's room. As soon as Mother closed the door, Vanessa threw herself on her bed and began sobbing into her pillow. While she was crying, thoughts were racing through her mind. *Why is it so wrong for a 9 year old not to like snow? I just don't like it, why doesn't anyone understand me? Everyone is different. Brandon doesn't like chicken, is he abnormal? Dad doesn't like pizza, is he abnormal? Mom doesn't like spicy food, is she abnormal? Who decides what "normal" is anyway?* Vanessa kept sobbing until she fell asleep.

22

****

The next morning, Vanessa was awoken by the sound of Brandon's loud mouth. "Oh man, look at all the snow outside! I bet ya the schools will be closed today, for sure!" Vanessa sprung up from her bed and looked out her window. Sure enough, her brother was right. There was a lot more snow outside than there was the day before. But Vanessa did not want to get her hopes up about school being closed, because every time she did, she was only disappointed. Vanessa made her way into the bathroom to get ready for school. When she passed the kitchen, she noticed her mother was fumbling with the radio dial. She hesitated for a moment before entering the bathroom. She was about to ask her mom if school was closed, but she decided not to. While Vanessa was brushing her teeth, she could hear her mother and Brandon talking. With the sound of the running water, however, she couldn't make out exactly what they were saying. Vanessa took a swig of water to rinse her mouth. She shut off the faucet. She listened. She nearly swallowed the water when she heard Brandon shout, "No way, Vanessa's school is closed and mine isn't! Aw man, that's no fair!"

Vanessa managed to lean forward over the sink to spit out the water from her mouth. She whipped open the bathroom door. She ran into the kitchen. "What did you say Brandon? Did you say that *my* school is closed today?"

A look of disgust sat on Brandon's face. He picked up his backpack and headed out the door.

Something to think about......

Has your school ever been closed because of snow or bad weather? What did you do on that day? Draw a picture of your memory from that day. Or, predict/draw what you think Vanessa might do.

Chapter 5
Home Alone

Mrs. Onero gave Vanessa a list of chores to do inside the house while she would be at work. "When the chores are complete, you can start working on your report for Mrs. Techlander."

Vanessa didn't know if she should feel happy or sad. She was happy that she didn't have to go to school, but she certainly didn't want to spend the day cleaning the house, or working on that dreadful report for Mrs. Techlander, which she never deserved in the first place.

As Mrs. Onero picked up her belongings to leave for work, she turned to Vanessa and said, "I'll call you from work to make sure everything is fine. I really hate leaving you home alone like this, but under the circumstances, there is nothing I can do." Mrs. Onero looked at Vanessa and said, "You'll be okay by yourself?"

Vanessa let out a sigh that signaled she was obviously annoyed, "Yeah Mom, I'll be fine. Don't worry, there's too much snow outside for the big bad wolf to come and get me."

"Okay dear, I'll try to be home as early as possible."

Just after Mrs. Onero shut the door behind her, Vanessa started running around the house. She jumped on the beds. She jumped on the couches. She jumped on just about every piece of furniture she could find. Vanessa made a decision to be happy about having the whole day and the whole house to herself.

First Vanessa decided to make herself some breakfast. Not just any old breakfast, but a celebrate-a-day-off-of-school-breakfast. Vanessa made chocolate chip pancakes, sausage, and freshly squeezed orange juice. Satisfied with her meal, she plopped herself down in front of the T.V. and flipped to the Nickelodeon channel. *Wow, this is great! Being off of school is so much fun. I better be careful not to spill on this couch!*

By the time she was finished with her celebrate-a-day-off-of-school-breakfast, the program was over. Vanessa brought her dish into the kitchen and took a look at the chore list. She figured that she could finish her chores quickly. That way, she could have time for fun things. Vanessa looked at the first chore on the list: wash dishes. So off she went to the sink. She poured soap into the dishpan. She rapidly scrubbed the dishes until they were squeaky clean. Done. The next chore on the list: vacuum the house. She went into the front hall closet to get the vacuum. She decided to start in her dad's home office and work her way through the rest of the house. Vanessa raced to plug in the vacuum and pushed it into the office. *If I keep working this fast, I'll have plenty of time for more fun things.* Vanessa started vacuuming the office. She quickly pushed the vacuum away from her and pulled it in. She got herself into a rhythm of push and pull, push and pull, push and pull, push and BUMP! OOPS! Vanessa hit the desk and a book fell on the floor. She stood the vacuum cleaner upright and shut it off. When she picked up the book, she noticed the title of it read, *World Wide Web Directory.* She read it again, this time out loud, "*World Wide Web Directory.*" Vanessa stopped to think what Mrs. Techlander had told them about the World Wide Web in class. She was thinking with all her brain, but she couldn't remember. If only she spent more time listening to Mrs. Techlander! Vanessa put the directory down and looked to see what else she could find. She suddenly remembered something very important. Her father told her she was not to go into his home office, or touch his new computer system. *Well,* Vanessa thought, *Mom gave me permission to be in here because I had to vacuum. I am not touching the computer. Technically, I'm not doing anything wrong.* Just then the phone rang.

Vanessa picked up the phone, "Hello."

"Vanessa, what *are* you doing?" Mrs. Onero didn't sound exactly calm.

Vanessa felt as if her mother were watching her on hidden camera or something. She swallowed hard and said, "Oh, hi Mom. I was just doing some of my chores."

"Why didn't you answer the phone before? I let it ring forever!"

"When did you try calling Mom?" Vanessa asked as she put the directory from her dad's office onto the table, which she began flipping through.

"Just a few minutes ago," Vanessa's mom sounded worried.

"Oh, I must have had the vacuum on Mom. I guess I didn't hear the phone. I can assure you that every thing is just fine here."

"Okay sweetie, I just wanted to check on you. I'll try calling again a bit later. Bye Nessa."

"Bye Mom." Vanessa hung up the phone and plopped herself down with the big directory. She was determined to find out more about this World Wide Web.

Something to think about......

Was Vanessa doing anything wrong in her dad's office?

Do you use the WWW and the Internet? I've included a page at the back of this book to list your favorite sites.

Chapter 6
Off Limits

Vanessa was overwhelmed by all the information in the big book she was flipping through. She couldn't quite understand any of it. She came to a page that said something about addresses. Each address started with the letters, WWW. This made absolutely no sense to Vanessa because her address was 4301 Brook Drive. She had never heard of an address that started with 3 W's before. Vanessa kept turning the pages of the big book. But, her efforts were useless. Vanessa was frustrated. She closed the book shut and placed it on her dad's desk where it was originally. Vanessa stood in front of the desk and stared at the new computer system. She was tempted to figure out how it worked. There was something stopping her. She had a flashback from the previous evening. She remembered her dad's strong green eyes looking through her meek brown ones. *Last, but not least, you are not allowed in my home office. I just had a new computer system installed, and it is absolutely off limits for you!* The phrase "off limits for you!" kept echoing in her head. For a moment, Vanessa thought she saw her father's face appear on the monitor. Her body shivered as if she were outside in the cold without any clothes on. That was enough to make Vanessa snap out of it. She double-checked that the directory was back in place. In haste, she got the vacuum and rolled it out of the office. When she rolled through the kitchen, she noticed that the clock read 12:30 p.m. *Wow! Time sure flies when I'm not in school!* Vanessa thought that she better get moving and vacuum the rest of the house. As Vanessa did the rest of the chores for the day, she decided that she wasn't going to get herself into any more trouble. She really didn't like it when everyone was mad at her.

When Vanessa finally finished all her chores on the list, it was 2:30 p.m. Brandon would be coming home from school soon if his basketball practice was cancelled. She was starting to get lonely in the house, so she decided to call her mom at work.

A secretary at her mom's office answered the phone, "Good afternoon, thank you for calling ABC Enterprises, this is Christine, how may I direct your call?"

Vanessa hated it when the secretary would babble on pretending that she was so happy to answer the phone. "Yes, I'd like to speak with Mrs. Onero please."

"One moment please," the secretary said cheerfully.

How could someone be so happy on a day with so much snow, Vanessa asked herself, as she waited for her mom to pick up the line.

"This is Mrs. Onero, how can I help you?"

"Hi Mom!"

"Oh, hi dear, is everything okay at home?"

"Yeah Ma, I just finished all of my chores. Now I am bored."

"Did you start on your report for Mrs. Techlander?"

Vanessa forgot all about that stupid report. "Uh, no. I really don't think I can do much until I get some books from the library."

"Well Vanessa, Brandon should be home any minute since he doesn't have basketball practice today. Have him help you. I have to attend a brief meeting. Then I'll be home."

"Sounds good Mom. Wait, I think I hear Brandon now. I'll see you later. Bye Mom."

"Bye Nessa."

Vanessa hung up the phone and ran to see if it was Brandon.

"Hey Brandon, how was your day?"

"Oh, it was fine. Even though school was open, a lot of kids didn't show up. The good thing is, I have no homework."

Brandon hung his coat and walked into the kitchen to get something to eat. Vanessa followed her brother into the kitchen like a lost puppy.

"Hey Brandon."

"What?"

Vanessa was being as polite as she could, "Do you think you could possibly help me out with my report after you finish eating?"

Brandon was so busy fixing himself a sandwich, that he didn't even hear what his sister said.

Vanessa was staring at Brandon, but he didn't respond. "Brandon, I said, do you think you could possibly help me with my report when you finish eating?"

"What report do you have? You didn't even go to school today."

"I got the assignment yesterday from Mrs. Techlander. Mom said that I should ask you to help me get started. Can you please?"

Brandon was busy stuffing his face, "Wul...I giss oo."

"Is that a yes or no?"

Brandon swallowed and said, "I guess so."

Vanessa felt grateful. She went to her room and gathered some paper and pencils. She wrote the word FLORIDA nice and big at the top of the paper. Vanessa went back into the kitchen and sat down at the table with Brandon.

"Okay sis, what kind of report do you have to write?"

"I have to write a ten-page researched report on Florida."

"Oh, I didn't know you had to do research. We only have one encyclopedia that would help you here. You really can't do much until you get to the library. But, I'll tell you what. I'll write down some major things you may want to include in your report. That should help you get a focus." Brandon wrote down some major categories on her paper: economy, government, history, and culture.

"Thanks Brandon. I really appreciate your help."

Brandon just gave Vanessa a weird look. He was trying to figure out why she was being so polite."

"Brandon?"

"What?"

"Do you think you can answer one more question I have?" Vanessa asked. Brandon nodded his head up and down. "What does it mean when an address has 3 W's in it?

"Vanessa, what in the world are you talking about?" Brandon looked perplexed.

"If I show you something, you promise not to tell?"

"Well, it depends on what it is."

"C'mon Brandon, just promise!"

"Fine Vanessa, what do you want to show me?"

Vanessa ran into her dad's office and took the big directory off the desk. She ran back into the kitchen, plopped the book on the table and flipped it open. She pointed to all the W's in the book and asked, "What do all these W's mean?"

Brandon just looked at Vanessa and giggled. "What are you doing with Dad's stuff?"

"Never mind. Answer my question."

"Well Vanessa, I can answer your question, but it won't do you any good. You are not allowed to use Dad's computer."

"What are you talking about? I just want to know what the W's stand for."

Brandon closed the directory and read the title to Vanessa out loud, *"The World Wide Web Directory."* Brandon repeated the words World Wide Web three times, and then he asked her what each of those words started with.

Vanessa was amazed, "Oh, WWW stands for World Wide Web, huh?"

"Bin-go!" said Brandon.

Vanessa again remembered that Mrs. Techlander talked about the World Wide Web during computer class, but Vanessa couldn't remember what she said. *Oh, if only I paid more attention in computer class. If I just paid more attention in school period, I wouldn't be in this predicament in the first place!*

In the meantime, Brandon went into the office and was sitting at the computer with his eyes glued to the screen. "Ohh, coooool!" he said with excitement.

Vanessa wanted to know what Brandon was doing. She found him in front of the computer. "What's soooo cooool?" she asked.

Brandon briefly explained that the addresses in the directory book are for the Internet. He could download tons of information. He was looking at some basketball stuff. It looked like some really tall guy was stuffing the basketball into the basket and the whole glass backboard shattered into a thousand pieces. "Oh, let me see. Oh, can I try, please, can I try? Oh please?" Vanessa begged.

Brandon just looked at Vanessa and laughed. "You have got to be dreaming, little sis. You aren't even allowed to touch this system. And besides, in order for you to use the web, you need to know the password to activate it.

Just because Brandon is older, he thinks he can tell her what to do! "Oh Brandon, please tell me what that password is, please!"

"You have got to be out of your mind. Remember yesterday, when you made me late for school? Well, it's payback time! I'm never gonna give you this password. You can sit here and beg all you want, but it's not gonna do you any good. I'm not going to reveal the secret password!" Brandon was satisfied that he could pay Vanessa back for what she did the day before. Brandon likes to get even.

Vanessa knew she had no chance to get that password from Brandon. She left the office and went into her room. *Who needs Brandon,* she thought, *I'll find a way to get that password on my own!*

Something to think about......

Have you ever had to do a major project for school?
What advice could you give to Vanessa to help her be
successful? If you'd like, you could write her a letter
below.

Dear Vanessa,

Chapter 7
Independence Day

The next day, Vanessa had to return to school. The snow stopped falling and the streets were cleared. *Today is Friday,* Vanessa thought, *I'm so glad the weekend is here.* There was something different about Vanessa that day. She felt different. She decided that she was going to turn over a new leaf. She was going to start paying more attention in school. If she had in the past, she would've been able to work that computer herself. She would've been able to figure out what the W's stood for. Vanessa was tired of depending upon other people. This day, she decided to declare her independence.

When Vanessa arrived at school, she discovered her class had computer lab in the morning. *Perfect. I can learn something from Mrs. Techlander, and go home and use that computer myself!*

"Good morning class, it's great to see everyone. I'm glad that we all survived the snowstorm." Mrs. Techlander was a bit too cheerful for Vanessa. But Vanessa remembered her "independence day", and dismissed her bad thoughts about Mrs. Techlander.

After Mrs. Techlander took care of the morning routine, she took the class down to the computer lab.

Vanessa took her assigned seat at station #17. She was never happier to sit at the computer. At least this computer was not "off limits" to her.

Once everyone was settled, Mrs. Techlander did some talking, as usual, about the assignment. Mrs. Techlander said that the class was going to explore the World Wide Web. Vanessa could hardly believe what she was hearing. When she heard the words: World Wide Web, her heart started pounding so hard, she thought it was going to jump right out of her chest. Just then, Vanessa raised her hand to tell Mrs. Techlander and the rest of the class something. Vanessa was holding her hand up and waving it around, she was beginning to get impatient. Vanessa didn't know why Mrs. Techlander didn't stop to call on her. *Maybe Mrs. Techlander needs to get better glasses. Maybe she can't see me. I am sitting near the back of the lab.* Vanessa was determined to get called on, so she kept waving her arm frantically in the air until Mrs. Techlander finally stopped talking and said, "Well Vanessa, it seems that you have something you want to ask me, what is it?"

"Well Mrs. Techlander, I just wanted to tell the class that the World Wide Web has a bunch of addresses in it and they all start with the letters WWW," Vanessa proudly said.

Mrs. Techlander gave Vanessa a smile and said, "You are exactly right Vanessa. And today, we are going to explore some of those addresses. If everyone could please look up at the board, you can see that I've listed a number of different sites that I'd like you to visit. You simply type in the address, exactly as you see it, and then press enter. Wait for a moment, and the site will appear on your screen. Look through the site and write down the following information: what kind of site it is, and two facts that you learned from the site. Any questions?" Mrs. Techlander looked around the lab. No one raised their hand so she let the class begin.

Vanessa was so excited. She was actually going to use the World Wide Web all by herself. It wasn't so hard. All she had to do was type in the address and the site would magically appear on the monitor. She didn't know why Brandon couldn't just tell her that the day before. Now she could go into the World Wide Web on the computer at home. But there were two obstacles. One, she didn't know the password. And two, she wasn't allowed to use the computer.

Vanessa enjoyed exploring the web, or "searching the web," as Mrs. Techlander put it. Mrs. Techlander was making her way around the lab to make sure everyone was on task. When she reached Vanessa's station, she praised Vanessa for sharing her comment with the class. Then she asked Vanessa if she had started on her report yet. Suddenly, Vanessa didn't like Mrs. Techlander any more.

Oh, yeah, Vanessa thought, *that stupid report. Where am I going to get all that information to fill ten whole pages?*

"The report? Uh, no. Actually, I'm having a little trouble finding lots of good information. Would you be able to give me any suggestions?"

Mrs. Techlander was pleased to hear Vanessa pose her question so politely. "Well Vanessa, I can write down some addresses for you to look up on the web. How does that sound?"

Vanessa couldn't believe that Mrs. Techlander was actually going to help her. Maybe she is human after all. "That would be great, if it's no problem for you."

"Oh no, I can jot down a few for you right now."

Vanessa kept searching the web. She was so fascinated by it that she didn't even care to socialize with her friends as she usually did during computer time.

Within a few minutes, Mrs. Techlander came back and gave Vanessa a slip of paper that had a few web addresses on it. "Thanks a lot Mrs. Techlander. I will have to look through these over the weekend on my computer at home."

For the first time this year, Vanessa was happy to be in school. Somehow it didn't seem so bad. She never thought she'd admit that learning could be fun in a strange kind of way.

Vanessa couldn't wait to look up the addresses Mrs. Techlander gave to her. Then she suddenly re-membered that she still didn't know the password to her dad's system. This didn't seem to bother her. She knew she would find a way to get the password some-how or another.

Something to think about......

Have you figured out why I chose to name Vanessa's teacher Mrs. Techlander? (pronounced: tek-land-er. Tech, like in technology!)

I use several "showing statements" throughout this story. I want to show you how Vanessa feels, instead of just telling you.
For example: Vanessa was excited. That is a telling statement. I am telling you how she felt.

Her heart was pounding so hard, she thought it was going to jump right out of her chest. That is a "showing statement." I am showing you how she felt. Perhaps you can remember a time when your heart felt this way.

See how many "showing statements" you can find while reading this story.

Chapter 8
Vanessa's Plan

That night, Brandon had a basketball game at his high school. Vanessa and her parents went to watch him play. Vanessa thought that her brother was a great basketball player. She was hopeful that his team would win. Vanessa enjoyed going to the high school games. She looked forward to the time when she would be in high school. She would like to be part of the dance team that performed during the half time shows.

Vanessa and her parents arrived just in time. They were announcing the starting line ups. "AND at point guard for your Wildcats is BRRRANDON ONERO!" The crowd went crazy cheering for Brandon. He was well-liked at his school.

The game was a close one, but the Wildcats won it by two points! Vanessa thought that close games were exciting, but they really made her nervous. Her brother was the one who scored the winning shot. Mr. and Mrs. Onero were so proud. Mrs. Onero actually had tears in her eyes when the game was over and the team was carrying Brandon on their shoulders. Brandon was the star of the game.

Even though Brandon can get on Vanessa's nerves sometimes, she still admired him and was very proud of him.

Vanessa and her parents went out to get a soda at the concession stand while waiting for Brandon to come out of the locker room. Vanessa gave her parents a summary of her day at school. She really emphasized that she liked working on the computer, with hopes that her dad would drop her punishment. "You know, if I had more time to practice on the computer, I bet I could get really good at it!"

"I bet you could Nessa. Good thing your school gives your class computer time every week. Otherwise, you may never have had a chance to work on one," Dad said with a grin on his face as he patted her on the back.

"Oh, here comes Brandon," Mrs. Onero shouted.

"Great game son! We are very proud of you!"

"Yeah, good game Brandon. You are lucky that your last shot went in!"

"No Vanessa, I'm not lucky, I just got skill!"

Brandon seemed like he was in a hurry. "Mom, Dad, the guys from the team want to go out to eat and celebrate. Could I use your car?"

"Sure honey, you can drop us off at home and take the car. Only if you promise not to stay out too late," Mrs. Onero said.

"It's a deal Mom. Let's go."

Vanessa couldn't wait until she was old enough to drive. She better stop getting in trouble now, so that by the time she gets her driver's license, her parents will let her borrow their car, too.

Brandon dropped his family off at home. "Thanks. I won't be too late."

Vanessa and her parents went inside the house. Mr. and Mrs. Onero decided that they were going to watch a movie for the remainder of the evening. Vanessa decided to read a book.

****

The next morning, Vanessa woke up later than usual. She was surprised to see the clock at 5 after 10. As Vanessa sat up in bed, she noticed that the book she was reading from the night before was now upside down on the floor. Vanessa didn't want to waste any time in bed. After all, it was Saturday. And for Vanessa, Saturday was "Funday." She decided to call her friend Erin and ask her to come over and play. Vanessa went into the kitchen to get the phone. Not to her surprise, her brother was babbling on it. Instead of making a fuss, Vanessa decided to eat her breakfast while she was waiting.

Brandon's room was right off the kitchen. When Vanessa ate breakfast, she always sat at the kitchen table in a chair that was closest to Brandon's room. There was only one reason why. She eavesdropped.

Vanessa peeked into Brandon's room before she sat down to eat. She couldn't help but notice that he looked quite upset. As Vanessa poured her milk into the cereal, she was wondering what could've happened to him. Vanessa just sat in her chair hoping she could hear something in her brother's conversation that would give her a clue. She put out her radar detectors to make sure she wouldn't miss a word of his conversation. "...I don't know man. This just really frustrates

49

me. What will I tell my parents? Isn't it gonna show up on the insurance or something?"

Vanessa didn't know exactly to whom Brandon was talking to, but it seemed like he was in some sort of trouble. Just then, Brandon looked out of his room and saw Vanessa sitting at the kitchen table. He gave her a dirty look and he closed the door to his room. Brandon usually closed his door when he was on the phone with his girlfriend, or when he didn't want anyone to know what he was talking about. Vanessa had a strong feeling that Brandon wasn't talking to his girlfriend. *Rats!* Vanessa thought, *Now how am I supposed to hear anything with that door closed!* Vanessa had to think quickly because a few seconds could cost her some very important gossip. She took a quick glance around the kitchen and noticed that the radio was on. Like lightening, she bolted out of her chair and turned it off. Vanessa glued her ear to Brandon's door. This is what she heard:

"I know, that cop was such a jerk! I wasn't going *that* fast. And besides, I didn't put anyone in any sort of danger or anything. Just 'cause the guy has a uniform, he thinks he is really something. You'd think he might have let me off, considering I won the game last night. Get that cop to play one-on-one with me, and I'll show him who's boss!"

Vanessa was so glad that she could hear. So far she understands that a cop stopped Brandon the night before for driving too fast. She pressed her ear to the door a little harder to hear more:

50

"...yeah, and since when does the law have the right to tell you that you *have* to wear a seatbelt? If I want to die in a car crash, that should be *my* right. I can't believe it! I have two tickets, no license *and* I have to go to court! How am I going to keep this from my parents?"

At that moment, Vanessa felt kind of bad for Brandon. She wondered if there was anything she could do. She walked away from Brandon's door and sat down to eat her cereal, which was now mush. She didn't know how much longer she should wait before asking Brandon for the phone. He was in such a bad mood, she didn't want to interrupt. Luckily, she didn't have to. Brandon opened his door and hung up the phone in the kitchen. Normally, Vanessa would've made a stink about how long he was on the phone, but she decided to back off this morning.

Vanessa put her cereal bowl in the sink and then called Erin.

Erin had this new computer game that she wanted to bring over by Vanessa's house, but since Vanessa was not allowed to use her father's computer, she had to go over to Erin's house. Vanessa wouldn't have minded so much if it weren't so darn cold outside. She put on so many layers that if she leaned too much to one side, she would've tipped over.

On her way to Erin's house, she came up with an absolutely brilliant idea. She did feel bad for what happened to Brandon and all, but there was something in it for her. She remembered hearing her brother say that he didn't know how he was going to keep this whole ticket/court thing from his parents. She wondered how badly Brandon did not want their parents to find out what happened. Vanessa decided that she would make her brother a deal. In order for Vanessa to keep quiet about the speeding incident, Brandon would have to give Vanessa the password for the computer.

When Vanessa arrived at Erin's house, she was so excited about her idea that she just had to share it with her friend. Erin wasn't at all surprised that Vanessa could come up with a plan to get what she wanted. Ever since Erin has known Vanessa, she has always gotten what she wanted.

While Vanessa and Erin were trying out Erin's new computer game, all Vanessa could think about was how she was going to confront Brandon with her deal. She couldn't just go into his room and demand the password because her mom would hear her. She had to be as discreet about this as possible. Vanessa decided that she would figure this out on her cold walk home. She seemed to do her best thinking while she was walking. In the meantime, Vanessa realized that she was losing the game against Erin. Vanessa is usually pretty competitive, but at that moment, she didn't care much. She had other things on her mind.

Before the girls knew it, it was time for Vanessa to leave. Once again, Vanessa had to get herself all bundled up for her venture home. As Vanessa was walking, she once again came up with a brilliant idea. She decided that she would write Brandon a contract, in which he would have to sign. She could slip it under his door and request that he write the password

52

down. His signature would make it official. He too, would have to discreetly leave the paper under her door. Vanessa was so excited about her idea, that she ran the rest of the way home.

Once Vanessa arrived at home, she removed all of her bulky winter attire and headed straight for her bedroom. She found a piece of her best stationary. It was cotton candy pink and had delicate flowers going across the top of the page. She thought for a moment. She wrote the following:

To Brandon Onero,

I know about the two tickets you got last night after the game. I also know that you do not have a license and that you have to go to court for speeding. We both know that it would break Mom and Dad's heart if they knew what you did. That's why I am not going to breathe a word of this to them, only under one condition. In exchange for me keeping my mouth shut, I want you to reveal the password for Dad's computer. They will never know that I got it from you. I will use the computer discreetly. If you are going to protect yourself, write the password below under your signature. If you decide not to take my offer, I will have to reveal the heartbreaking news to Mom and Dad. I will give you 24 hours to make your decision. Either way, please leave this paper under my closet door.

Signature_____
Password _____

Vanessa proudly folded her proposal and put it in her sock drawer until she knew it was safe to leave it under Brandon's door. She decided to leave her room to see what the rest of her family was up to. When she saw her mother all dressed up, she remembered that her mom and dad had a wedding to go to. She knew that meant one of two things. Either Brandon was going to stay in with her, or her grandmother was going to come over. Vanessa took one look at her mom and exclaimed, "Wow Mom! You really look great! I like it when you get all dressed up."

Mr. Onero was sitting in the living room waiting for his wife. "Vanessa could you please come here a minute?"

In an instant, Vanessa was in the living room. "Yes Dad, what is it?"

"Well, you know that your mother and I are about to go to a wedding. Your grandmother will be here any minute to stay with you until we get home. I expect you to behave. You have already gotten yourself into enough mishap."

"Oh Dad, you have nothing to worry about. I promise."

Mr. Onero got up from his chair to see if his wife was ready. Within a few minutes, Vanessa's parents were gone and her grandmother arrived. Vanessa ran to her room to get the note for Brandon. Brandon's door was closed when Vanessa went to his room. He was probably on the phone again. *Perfect*, Vanessa thought, *I'll just slip this under his door right now.* Vanessa quickly put the paper under the door and gave it a nice shove. She proceeded into the living room where her grandmother was taking off her coat.

"Hi Grandma. Why don't you come into the kitchen so that we could play cards for a while."

Vanessa's grandmother agreed. Vanessa enjoyed playing cards with her grandmother, even though her grandma always seemed to win. They both sat down at the kitchen table about to begin a game of Korichina. Korichina is a card game that Grandma taught Vanessa as soon as she was old enough to add. Each player must match or add facing numbers to cards in their hands. When all the cards run out, each player gets points based on how many and which cards they collected. They always played up to twenty-one points. Vanessa secretly thought that since her grandmother taught her the game, maybe she didn't quite teach her everything. Maybe that is why Grandma always seems to win. As Vanessa was shuffling the cards, Brandon whipped open his door. Their eyes locked. Brandon had a look of defeat on his face. Vanessa saw that he was holding the pink paper in his hand.

Their grandmother broke the silence. "Well, hello dear! Don't you look nice tonight. Do you have a date?"

Brandon smiled and said, "Well thanks Grandma, and yes I do have a date."

Vanessa couldn't take her eyes off the pink paper. She had to know if he put the password on it or not. Brandon went into Vanessa's room. When he came out, he was no longer holding the pink paper. Vanessa could hardly keep her mind on the card game. Brandon said good-bye and walked out the front door. Vanessa's grandma seemed to be enjoying Korichina. All Vanessa could think about was that pink piece of paper.

Something to think about......

What does Vanessa's stationary look like? Make a sketch, which includes your prediction about Brandon's reply.

Vanessa and her grandmother are playing a game called Korichina. To play, you need a regular deck of playing cards and 2-4 players.

Designate one player as the dealer for the game (you can switch off). Each player gets four cards. Place four cards face up on the table. There are two ways to pick up cards from the table. You can match the card itself (an 8 with an 8, or a king with a king). Another way to pick up cards is to add cards on the table to one in your hand. For example, if you have a 7 in your hand you could pick up a 1 and 6, or a 2 and 5, or a 3 and 4 from the table. If nothing in your hand matches or adds up to the cards on the table, you need to place one of your cards on the table. Keep alternating turns until all four cards from the players' hands are gone. The dealer then deals four more cards to each player. Keep repeating this sequence until the dealer has run out of cards. Once the dealer has run out of cards, it is time to count points from what you have gathered. The points are as follows:

Player with the most cards	2 points
Player with the most clubs	1 point
Player with the 10 of diamonds	1 point
Player with the 2 of clubs	1 point

Keep track of your points. The first one to get 21 points wins!

Chapter 9
The Pink Paper

"Excuse me Grandma, I'll be right back." Vanessa shot up from her chair and zipped to her room. If she had to wonder about Brandon's decision any longer, she would've had a nervous breakdown. Grandma Onero dropped the playing cards and caught a glimpse of her before she disappeared out of sight. "Oh my," Grandma said to herself, "I didn't know that Vanessa was training for the Olympic track team!"

Vanessa closed her bedroom door behind her. Her heart was pounding like a caffeinated jumping bean. Vanessa took four deliberate steps to reach her closet door. She slowly inhaled through her nose and exhaled through her mouth. She wiped her palm against her jeans before she gripped the door handle. Each finger hugged the handle tightly. At a snail's pace, she pulled the door open. Vanessa stood at the edge of her closet like a stone. She lowered her eyes to the floor. Her eyes froze when they met the pink paper, which was folded in half. Vanessa could not let time stand still. She had to know if she had the password or not. She bent down, picked up the paper and opened it with a quick, shaky hand. When she looked at the last line, she jumped so high off the ground that she took a short trip to the moon and back. When Vanessa reached Earth again, her heart was pounding uncontrollably. All of a sudden, she heard her grand-ma knock on her door. "Nessa, what are you doing in there?"

Vanessa was so excited about the pink paper that she had forgotten that her grandmother was over. Vanessa quickly folded the pink paper and put it in the back pocket of her jeans. When she opened the door, her grandmother had a puzzled look on her face. "What kind of trouble are you getting yourself into now?"

"Who me?" Vanessa asked as if she had never gotten into trouble before.

Grandma Onero looked behind her and all around and said, "Yes you. I don't see anyone else here."

"Oh Grandma, you always think I'm up to no good. To be honest, I just had to run into my room to jot something down in my journal. I had to write it down before I forgot. And since it is kind of personal, I can't share it with you."

"That's fine dear." Grandma Onero shook her head, turned away from Vanessa's room and headed back towards the kitchen. Vanessa skipped quietly behind her grandmother with a plan in mind. "Grrraaaandma, " Vanessa said in her sweetest voice.

"Yes dear."

"Would you like me to make you some tea before we continue playing cards again?"

"Oh Vanessa, I could really use a nice cup of hot tea now. Thank you."

Vanessa filled up the tea kettle and set it on top of the stove. She took out her grandmother's favorite mug. It had delicate angels on it. Vanessa had a couple of teas to choose from: Lipton or a gourmet tea called Sleepytime. Without hesitation, Vanessa took out a Sleepytime tea bag and placed it in the angel mug. Soon enough, the water was ready. Vanessa served her grandmother the tea and they began a new game of Korichina. Vanessa was content with this game because she was sitting on the password to her father's computer. She was planning to test it out the first safe chance she could get.

Without surprise, Grandma Onero won the card game. Vanessa could never quite figure out how Grandma did it. "Okay Grandma, I want to challenge you to one more game. I know I can win!"

"Oh sweetie, maybe we can play later. Right now I would like to go into the living room and take a rest."

"I understand. We can play later."

Grandma went into the living room to lie down on the couch. Vanessa put the cards away and straightened up the kitchen. When Vanessa went into the living room to check on her grandmother, she was sound asleep. Vanessa put her hand in front of her grandmother's nose, just to make sure she was still breathing. *Wow! That Sleepytime tea sure does work fast!* Before another minute expired, Vanessa dashed into her dad's office. She found that the computer was on with its screen saver. She frantically shook the mouse to get rid of the screen saver. A big white box appeared on the screen that read: PLEASE ENTER YOUR PASSWORD. There was a smaller rectangular box inside the big one with a blinking cursor. *Oh, I guess this is where I'm supposed to type in my password,* Vanessa thought to herself. In haste, she took out the pink paper to be sure she typed in the password, exactly as Brandon had written it. Vanessa typed each letter carefully. N O L I M I T S. All of a sudden, the screen changed. It now showed the Internet! Vanessa rubbed her eyes and looked at the screen again. She was in awe. *I can't believe it! I really have the password!* Vanessa was so excited; she didn't know what to do with herself next. She could look in the *World Wide Web Directory* to get some ideas or she could use those addresses that Mrs. Techlander gave her. At this point, all that really mattered to Vanessa was that she had access to the system. Vanessa decided that she would go and get the addresses that Mrs. Techlander gave her. As Vanessa was walking back to her room, she noticed that her grandmother was no longer sleeping. Vanessa made an about face and went back into her dad's office to turn off the computer. She now realized that she was going to have to come up with a plan to use the computer without getting herself caught.

Something to think about......

What do you suppose the password (NoLimits) means?
Do you think Vanessa's dad chose this for a reason?
What kind of password would you use for your own computer system?
What does it say about you?

Enter
Password:

Chapter 10
The Unfinished Report

The next morning, Vanessa's mother woke her up to go to church. Vanessa and her mom go to church just about every Sunday. And once in a while, Brandon would go, too. After church, Mrs. Onero usually takes Vanessa to their favorite pancake house. This Sunday, however, was a little different.

"Aw, c'mon Mom. You always take me for pancakes on Sunday!"

"I'm sorry honey. You can eat something at home and work on your report for Mrs. Techlander for the rest of the afternoon." Mrs. Onero knew that Vanessa was disappointed.

"What?" Vanessa sounded shocked. "You mean you are going to lock me into my room and force me to do my report for the rest of the day?"

Mrs. Onero couldn't help but let out a laugh. "Oh Vanessa, you are so dramatic."

"Mom, haven't you learned anything from all those years of attending church? Sunday is a holy day and no one should work on Sundays. How does that saying go in church vocabulary?" Vanessa firmly pressed her lips together as she tilted her head to one side to find the words she was looking for. "I know," Vanessa said, "And on the Seventh Day God rested. See Mom, if God rested on Sundays, then that means I should, too." Vanessa stood beside her mom with her arms folded across her chest.

Mrs. Onero smiled at Vanessa and told her, "Nessa, I'm happy to see that you have learned something in Sunday school, but it is not going to work. You still have to go home and do your report. Without another word, Vanessa got into the car with her mom. Vanessa remained silent the whole way home.

After Vanessa and her mom arrived at home and ate lunch, Vanessa had an idea. "Mom, do you think I could work on my report at the library instead? I think I could concentrate better there."

Mrs. Onero looked at Vanessa and said, "Well, I suppose so. I'll clean up, and you can get yourself ready to go."

"Okay Mom, I'll go get ready." Vanessa really didn't enjoy going to the library, but she figured she'd rather be in the library where her mother couldn't hover over her every five minutes.

When Vanessa arrived at the library, it was 1:30 p.m. She wasn't going to be picked up until 4:30 p.m. There was a lot of work to be done. Her report was due in three days and she hadn't even started it yet.

With the help of the librarian, Vanessa gathered encyclopedias and other books pertinent to her report. She started to read and take notes. It didn't take long however, before Vanessa was distracted. She noticed that some of the computers in the library were hooked up to the Internet. Vanessa shuffled through her notebook to find the addresses that Mrs. Techlander gave her. She found the closest librarian and asked for Internet access. To her disappointment, Vanessa was told that she must have an adult with her in order to use the computer. Vanessa went back to her table and sulked. She no longer had any motivation to work on her stupid report. Vanessa looked at the clock and realized she still had an hour and a half left before she could go home. She decided to get a magazine. Once she finished looking at one, she got another. Vanessa was bored. She thought about what she could do that would be more interesting. *I got it! I can devise a plan to use Dad's computer without getting into trouble.* Vanessa frantically began writing down everyone's schedules in her house. She wrote down the times they woke up, left the house, returned to the house, went to sleep, and anything else they did in between. After all of her hard work, she came to the conclusion that the only really safe time to use the computer would be in the middle of the night, while everyone was sound asleep.

In order for Vanessa's plan to work well, she jotted down some important tips. Her tips included the following: 1) Close the door to the office *before* turning the computer on. 2) Place a towel up against the bottom of the door to prevent any light from escaping out. 3) Turn the volume all the way down *before* turning on the computer. 4) Be sure to leave the office exactly as it was found.

Vanessa felt very satisfied with her plan. She felt confident enough to try it out that night. Soon enough, it was time for Vanessa to pack her things up to go home. She checked out a few books about Florida so that her mom would think she was being somewhat productive.

****

That night, Vanessa told her parents that she was going to bed a little earlier than usual. She looked over her plan once again. She waited. She waited until she knew that everyone in the house was asleep. Vanessa's heart was pounding so hard; she was hoping that the sound of it wouldn't wake anyone up. She took the Internet addresses that Mrs. Techlander gave her and quietly left her room. She peeked her head into her parents' room to make sure they were both sound asleep. She continued to scamper like a mouse throughout the dark apartment and into the forbidden room. She followed her plan exactly as written. She entered the password: NoLimits. She was on her way to the Internet. She was working as quietly as she could, while exploring the sites that Mrs. Techlander had given her. But somehow, Vanessa wasn't too thrilled. The Internet was better than using the encyclopedias, but Vanessa realized she still had to generate a ten-page report somehow with all this information. The excitement had worn off. She had conquered doing something she wasn't supposed to do. She looked at the clock. It was 2:00 a.m. She had to get up for school in a matter of hours. She shut down the computer and went to bed. She was disappointed that her late night Internet session hadn't been more adventurous.

When Vanessa went under the covers, she dreamed about having wings. Wings that could take her anywhere she wanted, whenever she wanted. If only she could have a pair of wings, she would be the happiest girl in the whole world.

Something to think about......

Vanessa feels that if she has wings, she will be the happiest girl in the world. She wants to feel carefree. What is something that makes you feel carefree? Draw a picture of it below.

Chapter 11
Late Night with Vanessa

When Vanessa arrived at school that morning, Mrs. Techlander asked her how her report was coming along. Vanessa really didn't want to be reminded of her report, especially that morning, since she was so tired from staying up late the night before. Somehow Vanessa managed to stay awake throughout the day. The thought of what Mrs. Techlander would do if she caught Vanessa sleeping in class, was enough for her to keep her eyes wide open.

When Vanessa got home, she took a nice nap until dinnertime. Vanessa was not in the best of moods, so she was a little crabby when she woke up.

"What happened to you?" Brandon asked as he looked at his sister.

"Leave me alone," Vanessa snapped.

"Are you feeling okay?" Mrs. Onero sounded concerned. "It's not like you to come home from school and go to sleep."

"I'm tired Mom. What's so bad about that?"

"Nothing dear. I just want to make sure that you aren't coming down with something."

"Ma, the only thing that would make me feel better right now is a pair of wings!"

Mrs. Onero and Brandon looked at each other in astonishment. Mrs. Onero asked, "What in the world are you talking about Nessa?"

Brandon added, "Yeah Vanessa, what's your problem?"

"Don't you guys understand? If I had a pair of wings, I could go anywhere I wanted, whenever I wanted!"

Mrs. Onero put her hand on Vanessa's forehead. "Let me see if you feel warm."

Vanessa pulled away from her mother. "I'm fine!"

Mrs. Onero called her husband, "John, please come here!"

Vanessa's father went into the kitchen and asked, "What's going on?"

"I don't know dear. I am really concerned about Vanessa. I think she could have the seasonal affective disorder. Do you think we should take her to a doctor?"

"What are you talking about?" Mr. Onero asked. Then he said, "I think we all need to just sit down and eat. Vanessa is fine."

Vanessa knew herself why she was so tired, but she wouldn't dare admit it to anyone. As Vanessa was eating, she began once again to think about the luxury of having wings. Deep down inside however, she knew that this was one thing she would not be able to devise a plan for. She had to accept the fact that human beings were just not designed to fly.

After dinner, Vanessa was watching her favorite T.V. program, when her mother reminded her, "Vanessa, I think you better get going on your report. You know it is due the day after tomorrow!" Vanessa obeyed her mom and went to her room to work on her Florida report. She began reading and taking notes at her desk. She thought she'd be more comfortable on her bed. She plopped herself on her bed and began to read. The words on the pages soon hypnotized her. She dozed off for a while and when she woke up, everyone else was sound asleep. Vanessa decided that she might be able to stay awake if she worked on the computer instead. She decided to go to her dad's office to begin web surfing. This time however, Vanessa wasn't filled with the same excitement as she was the night before. Without a problem, she followed her tips sheet and was set up in the office in no time. She visited a Florida site and took down some notes. She visited another Florida site and took down some more notes. Vanessa was bored. She wanted to play around with the web to see if she could find more interesting sites.

At first, Vanessa took her dad's *World Wide Web Directory* and started flipping through it. All she found was a bunch of addresses that had no meaning to her. Vanessa shut the directory in disappointment. She folded her hands on top of the book and put her head down. *How did I get myself into this mess? I just want to go to sleep and when I wake up, I want it to be summer! At least in the summer, there isn't any school and there aren't any teachers like Mrs. Techlander to assign ridiculous reports.* Vanessa forced herself to pick up her head and look at the monitor. *Wow,* she thought, *these pictures of the palm trees and the ocean are great, but they don't make me feel any better. If only I could be there. If only I had wings to get me there right now!*

Vanessa felt like taking the whole computer system and throwing it out the window. Instead, she took her frustration out on the keyboard. She pressed both hands on the keyboard as hard as she could. The monitor displayed the following: SITE NOT FOUND. Vanessa pounded on the keyboard again and again, only for the monitor to display: SITE NOT FOUND. Vanessa deleted all the nonsense letters she pounded in. She decided that she wanted to invent her own address. She typed in WWW.WINGS. Within a moment, the computer read: SITE IS BUSY. PLEASE WAIT. Vanessa rapidly began pressing the return key and clicking the mouse hoping to speed up the waiting process. All of a sudden, the screen turned blank. Vanessa felt as if her whole body turned into a popsicle. *Oh my gosh! What did I do? I'm dead.* Vanessa couldn't do anything but stare at the blank screen, which was now beginning to turn black. She didn't quite know what was happening to the computer, but she was sure she broke it. She began to breathe heavily in panic. *What am I going to do? My dad is gonna kill me!* Vanessa got up from the chair and turned her back away from the computer. She took a deep breath and thought, *I'm sure it's nothing. I'm going to just turn around and restart the computer. That is probably all I need to do. Just turn around and restart the computer.*

When Vanessa turned around to restart the computer, her eyes bulged out of their sockets and her chin dropped to the floor. She couldn't believe what had happened. The computer screen now had green neon writing on top of the black screen. This is what she saw.

YOUR DREAM IS ABOUT TO COME TRUE. FOLLOW
THESE STEPS.

1) PLACE BOTH HANDS UP TO THIS SCREEN.

2) CLOSE YOUR EYES.

3) THINK OF SOMEPLACE YOU WANT TO BE
   RIGHT NOW.

4) COUNT TO 10.

Vanessa read what she saw on the screen more than once. She didn't know if someone was playing a trick on her or not, but she didn't see any harm in trying it out. Vanessa followed the directions on the screen very carefully. The last thing she remembered was counting to 3 or 4. She felt an electric shock, first in her hands, and then throughout her body. After that, she was sucked up like a vacuum. How? She was not so sure. When Vanessa opened her eyes, she had to shut them again. It took a few moments for her to scope out her surroundings. The first thing she noticed was the scorching sun beating on her. The palm trees, the sand, the boats, the waves; it was all so beautiful. Vanessa absolutely couldn't believe this was really real. She had to pinch herself several times to make sure that she wasn't dreaming. Once she realized where she was, she felt a little uncomfortable in her nightgown. But she didn't let that stop her from enjoying her surroundings. She had been longing for the hot sun for weeks. Vanessa sprinted through the blazing sand and into the ocean. The waves knocked up against her knees. Vanessa just stood in awe, until someone called out to her, "Hey kid, what are you sleepwalkin' or somethin'?" Vanessa ignored the comment and got out of the water. *If I had known I was coming here, I would've been more prepared. I wonder how long I will be here. I wonder how I will get back. Will I get back?*

Vanessa saw a large group of kids about her age nearby. She decided to see what they were up to. As she got closer, she noticed some of the kids looking at her funny. They were whispering to one another and giggling. Vanessa didn't care, because she got close enough to hear one of the adults talking about their trip to Disney World for the next day. *That's where I really want to go! If I get the chance, I'll come back tomorrow.* Vanessa didn't care about anyone around her. All she knew was that by some miracle, she was where she had dreamed to be. She decided to sit in the sand and absorb as much sun as possible. Vanessa had a feeling that she wouldn't be in paradise forever.

Soon after Vanessa sat in the sun, she fell asleep. When she woke up, she was disappointed to find herself in front of her dad's computer. Vanessa stared at the screen in wonder.

Something to think about......

Vanessa's mom is worried that her daughter could have SAD. SAD (Seasonal Affective Disorder) can occur in the winter months, when people are affected by the lack of sunlight. If someone has SAD they have difficulty going about their daily routines. What is your opinion? Do you think that Vanessa has SAD?

Do you think that Vanessa really experienced "computer magic?" why or why not?

Chapter 12
Tomato Face

"Good morning Vanessa."

Vanessa managed to wave to her mom in the kitchen as she went into the bathroom. Vanessa felt as is her whole body were moving in slow motion. She got herself washed up as quickly as possible. She didn't dare want to make Brandon late for school. When Vanessa finished washing up, she went into the kitchen for a quick breakfast. Her mom looked at her in a peculiar way. "Your breakfast is on the table Nessa."

"Thanks Mom."

Mrs. Onero took her cup of coffee and sat down at the table with Vanessa. She couldn't help but stare at Vanessa's face. "Nessa?"

"Yeah."

"Why is your face so red?"

"My face?" Vanessa replied.

"Yes Vanessa, your face," Mrs. Onero sounded a little agitated.

Vanessa hadn't realized that her face was *that* red. She had to come up with a believable answer, quick. "Oh, I must have scrubbed a little too hard with the washcloth. My skin is rather dry and all because of the harsh weather." Vanessa wouldn't dare tell anyone about her experience from the night before.

They would think she was absolutely insane. Vanessa's mom sighed and said, "If you say so dear. Please put your dishes on the sink and get your coat on. I don't want you to be late for school."

"Will do."

As Vanessa grabbed her coat from the front hall closet, she took a look at her face in the mirror on the door. Her face looked like someone smeared tomatoes all over it and put it in the oven. *Wow! I must have been out in the sun for quite a while. I wonder what I'm going to tell all the kids as school. I'd love to tell them where I went last night, but I doubt that anyone would believe me.* Vanessa quickly put her coat on and ran out to the car where her mother was waiting.

When Vanessa arrived at school, a lot of kids gathered around her and were staring at her face. *Just great. What am I going to tell them?* Soon enough, Mrs. Techlander shoved everyone into the classroom and took a look at Vanessa. "What in the world happened to you Vanessa?"

"Oh, I don't know Mrs. Techlander. I could be allergic to the cold weather. My skin is rather sensitive. I'm sure it will go away." Vanessa has never been allergic to anything in her whole life, but Mrs. Techlander seemed to believe her.

"Well Vanessa, it does look like you have sensitive skin. Go down to the nurse and have her put some soothing cream on it for you."

Vanessa went to the nurse. She hated the way the cream smelled. Vanessa thought she was going to be sick. She decided that if she goes to Florida again, she would definitely put some sunblock on her face to prevent it from getting any more sunburned than it already was.

When Vanessa went back to class, Mrs. Techlander called her up to her desk. "Vanessa, how are you feeling?"

"I'm fine. The nurse put this smelly cream on my face."

Mrs. Techlander looked at Vanessa's face and seemed satisfied that there was cream on it. "Good. Now let's talk about business. How is your Florida report coming along?"

"My report? Uh, it's fine."

"Well, don't forget, it's due tomorrow. You will have to share some of it with the class. I expect you to come to school prepared."

"Yes Mrs. Techlander. I will be prepared for tomorrow." Vanessa smiled at her teacher, but she really felt like knocking her off her desk chair. Vanessa went back to her desk and wondered how her sleep deprived self would pull off getting the report done in one night.

Soon enough, it was time for P.E. Vanessa was sure to line up next to her friend Erin. She couldn't wait to tell Erin what she did the night before. Vanessa whispered to Erin, "I've got a secret to tell you."

Erin loved secrets. "What is it?" she whispered.

"Girls," Mrs. Techlander said in a firm voice. "Is there something you'd like to share with the rest of us?"

Vanessa and Erin just shook their heads and got in line.

Once they reached the gym, Erin asked Vanessa, "So what is this secret you have for me?"

Vanessa replied, "It is top secret. I don't want anyone else to hear a word of it. We'll have to wait until after school.

Erin was disappointed. She hated to wait. She especially hated to wait when she was waiting for a top secret, secret.

The day at school went fast, even though everyone kept staring at Vanessa's face and Erin kept bugging Vanessa about her secret. Before Vanessa left, Mrs. Techlander reminded her once again about her report being due the next day. Vanessa didn't leave school on a very happy note. She knew she had tons of work to do when she got home. Vanessa avoided Erin by taking an alternative route out of the building and to her mom's car. She no longer felt like sharing her top secret, secret.

Something to think about......

Vanessa was out in the sun without any protection. If she had sunblock on, she wouldn't have gotten burnt.

Design a sun protection product and write an advertisement below.

Chapter 13
The All Nighter

When Vanessa came home from school, she found a piece of paper folded in half on top of her desk. *Now what? I have enough things to worry about.* Vanessa looked at the piece of lined notebook paper. She recognized that her name was written in Brandon's handwriting. Vanessa's pulse started to rise. *Great. What does he want?* Vanessa opened up the note and read:

I DON'T KNOW WHEN YOU ARE USING DAD'S COMPUTER, BUT IF YOU GET CAUGHT, YOU BETTER NOT TELL MOM OR DAD HOW YOU GOT THE PASSWORD. AFTER YOU READ THIS, CUT IT UP IN LITTLE PIECES AND THROW IT AWAY!!!

Vanessa wondered for a moment how Brandon knew. The note however, didn't worry Vanessa one bit. She was sure that she wasn't going to get caught. She tore up the paper in little pieces and threw it away, just as Brandon requested. Now she had to move on to more important things, like the ten-page report, which was hardly started.

Vanessa took out her spiral and put her name at the top. She thought for a moment and wrote the words "Florida Report" on the top of her page. Vanessa read over her notes she had taken, but she had no idea on how to begin the actual writing of the report. She decided to put her work aside. She thought a good snack would stimulate her thinking. Vanessa went into the kitchen and had a sandwich and some chips. She decided to then stay in the kitchen to help her mother cook. "What are you making for dinner tonight Mom?"

"I am making your dad's favorite, spaghetti with homemade meat sauce," replied her mom.

"Do you mind if I help?"

"Well, I am almost done with the sauce, but you can start cutting up the salad if you'd like."

"I don't mind." Vanessa would rather do anything besides that stupid report. As Vanessa was tearing apart the lettuce and putting it into a bowl, her mother asked the question Vanessa was hoping to avoid, "Nessa, isn't your report for Mrs. Techlander due tomorrow?"

"Yeah Mom. I am almost done with it. I will finish the rest after dinner."

"Good. I just wanted to make sure. Mrs. Techlander will be quite upset if you hand in an unfinished report. Are you sure you don't need my help with any of it?"

"Don't worry Mom. I have everything under control."

****

After dinner, Vanessa excused herself from the table and told her parents she would be in her room finishing her report, even though she was really just beginning. Vanessa sat on her bed with her spiral notebook. She took out all the notes she had. She forced herself to generate some sentences from them. Before long, Vanessa had two pages written front and back. Her report however, had to be typed. So in reality, she only had two pages out of ten completed. She couldn't even consider herself halfway done. *When is this going to end! I absolutely hate reports! Hate 'em, hate 'em, hate 'em!!!* Vanessa needed a break. She put her head on her pillow and took a nap. When she woke up, it was time to go on the computer.

She decided that she was going to take her adventure first, and she would finish her report when she got back. This was logical. After all, if she made it to Florida, she could get more information for her report. Vanessa made her way into the office. She was good to go and booted up the computer. After entering the password, Vanessa began to get excited. She knew where she was heading, and she knew it would be fun. All of a sudden, she remembered she was still in her nightgown. She went back into her room to put on her bathing suit. Knowing that she might not only be at the beach, she put on a pair of shorts and tank over her suit. Next she went into the bathroom and managed to find some sunblock. She applied the sunblock all over her body. Vanessa tiptoed her way out of the bathroom. She poked her head into her parents' room just to make sure they were sound asleep. She couldn't see much because it was dark, but she could hear her dad snoring. That was a sure sign he was in a deep sleep.

When Vanessa went back into the office, she had to retype the password. At the prompt she entered, WWW.WINGS. Every part of Vanessa's body was dancing. When it came time for Vanessa to put her hands up to the screen and close her eyes, she took a deep breath. She envisioned herself at Disney World and began counting slowly to ten. Once again she felt a small electric shock in her hands first and then throughout her body. When she opened her eyes, she saw a huge castle. Vanessa spun around. She felt as if she were flying. She couldn't remember a time in her life in which she was happier than she was at that very moment. *Wow! I can't believe that I'm really here! Oh look, there's Mickey Mouse, my favorite. I better get a picture with him, so I can show everyone at home.* Vanessa ran up to Mickey Mouse and gave him a big hug. Suddenly she realized that she didn't have a camera with her, nor did she have any money to buy one. *Oh well, I will remember this day forever; I don't really need a picture.* Vanessa wanted to absorb as much of the surroundings as she could. She didn't know at what moment she would find herself back at her dad's computer. Vanessa shook hands and hugged every one of the Disney characters, including: Mickey, Minnie, Donald and Goofy. Before she knew it, smoke of vibrant colors started shooting up from the base of the stage. *Gee, I guess they want to get everyone's attention. Looks like a show is about to begin.* Vanessa ran closer to the stage. Her heart was beating in sync with the lively music. Dancers came out onto the stage one by one wearing awesomely decorated costumes. Vanessa began dancing to the beat of the music as she watched the show. More and more people started to gather around as the show went on. Vanessa was annoyed with the little boy who was standing next to her. All he did was whine about how he wanted to go to the haunted house. His mother couldn't listen to him anymore, so she yanked his arm and pulled him out of the crowd. Vanessa had a feeling they were going to the haunted house. She decided to follow them.

Ordinarily, Vanessa would've been a little scared. But not this time, she was too happy to let anyone or anything scare her. She waited in line behind the little brat and his mom. Before long, Vanessa entered the haunted house. It was midnight black inside. At first, Vanessa was fine. But after a few minutes, her imagination began to take its toll. She went into one room in which it felt like the floor beneath her had dropped. Her heart dropped right down to her heels, up to her chin, down to her stomach and back up into place. Vanessa wasn't so sure she wanted to be inside the haunted house anymore. She managed to find a security guard who let her out a side door. Once Vanessa was out in the light, she felt a little better. She wondered how the boy who was younger than her was able to handle it.

Vanessa began walking. Her walk turned into a joyful skip. Where she was headed, she did not know, nor did she care. All she knew was that WWW.WINGS had taken her to where she wished to go! She saw a group of boys and girls that looked like they were about her age. She decided to follow along behind them. She overheard they were on their way to ride

Space Mountain. *That's what I want to do! I want to go on a ride!* Vanessa skipped along behind the group with a smile on her face. She was sure she was going to enjoy Space Mountain. She loved rides. Once Vanessa was in line for the ride, she discovered that this roller coaster was like no other roller coaster she had ever been on before. Space Mountain rode in the dark. All of a sudden, Vanessa broke out into a cold sweat. She thought she was going to faint. *The dark? Isn't that dangerous? Couldn't somebody fall out?* Vanessa was next in line. She didn't know what to do. She asked the attendant, " Exactly how fast does this ride go?"

The ride attendant looked at Vanessa and smirked. "Are you scared kid?"

Vanessa felt like punching the guy. "Well, I'm just concerned about falling out of the car. As you can see, I'm not a very big person. And besides, if I did fall out, no one would know because the ride is in the dark."

"You have nothing to worry about kid. Your car is here. Are you in or out?"

"I'm in," Vanessa said as she jumped into the car.

Vanessa strapped herself in and said a little prayer before the ride began. Vanessa had no idea what to expect. She was scared. She couldn't believe that she waited in line to be scared like that. Once the ride began, Vanessa held onto the bar in front of her so tight, that she thought her fingers were going to fall off. The roller coaster made a few turns left and right and left and right. Then it began climbing up.

Vanessa's heart began pounding faster and faster. Because it was dark, she didn't know when it was going to drop. She could hear the cranking of the wheels as the roller coaster was going higher and higher. When she heard the wheels slow down and come to a halt, she held onto the bar even tighter. Sure enough, the roller coaster took a sudden drop. Piercing screams broke the dark silence. The roller coaster took a few whizzing turns left and right. The power of the turns shifted Vanessa's body from right to left in the car. The roller coaster seemed to be picking up speed. Vanessa didn't dare take her hands off the bar in front of her. Suddenly Space Mountain took a quick drop down and Vanessa's bottom took a quick leap up. Space Mountain picked up even more speed as it went through a tunnel. Vanessa couldn't see anything, but she shut her eyes anyway. When Vanessa opened her eyes, her hands were tightly holding the keyboard. The monitor in front of her displayed its screen saver.

Vanessa's chest was rising and falling quite rapidly. Vanessa took her hands off the keyboard and turned away from the computer. *What in the world has happened to me? How am I all of a sudden back again? I'm not so sure that I like having wings.* Vanessa's breathing came to a normal pace within a few minutes. She looked at the clock, alarmed to see that it read 4:30 a.m. Vanessa couldn't believe it! She started to panic. *What am I going to do? My report is due in a matter of hours and it is not close to being finished!* Suddenly Vanessa had an idea. She situated herself in front of the computer again. She shook the mouse frantically to get rid of the screen saver. At the

91

prompt she punched in the password. Vanessa decided to make up her own web address once again. She typed in WWW.FLORIDA.REPORT. After a few moments, the screen displayed, SITE NOT FOUND. Vanessa tried another address: WWW.VANESSA.FLORIDA.REPORT. Once again, the screen displayed, SITE NOT FOUND. Vanessa was sure that she had some kind of computer magic. After all, she did discover WWW.WINGS. *Think Vanessa. There's gotta be an address that will get that report done. Computers can do anything now a days.* Vanessa hopefully punched in a few more fictitious addresses. To her dismay, none were valid.

Vanessa felt like crying. She held back, for fear that everyone would wake up. She didn't know how she was going to explain this to Mrs. Techlander. The only option she had would be to simply tell the truth. Instead of trying to make up some crazy story, Vanessa decided that she was going to tell the truth for once. She was going to tell Mrs. Techlander and the class about her adventure on WWW.WINGS.

Something to think about......

Design a room in a haunted house. What makes it so
haunted? Draw you room below.

Chapter 14
Vanessa's Report

"Vanessa...Vanessa...Vanessa...VA-NES-SA!" Mrs. Onero called out from the kitchen. Vanessa was in bed and did not budge. Mrs. Onero went into Vanessa's room and began shaking her daughter. "Come on Vanessa, it's time to get up."

Vanessa felt her mother shaking her, but had no energy what so ever to move out of her bed. She felt as if she had been run over by a truck. "I'm tired Mom."

"Oh no, Vanessa. You can't pull one today. Today you have to give your report. Now get out of bed. I prepared breakfast for you."

Vanessa forced herself to swing both of her legs over to one side of the bed and push herself up with her hands. *Wow, three hours certainly go by fast when you are sleeping!* Vanessa could smell pancakes and bacon in the kitchen. She began walking to the kitchen, but decided to detour to the bathroom. Vanessa ran the cold water and splashed some on her face, hoping she would feel alive. The cold water made her open her eyes a little wider, but did nothing for the hit-by-a-truck feeling her body had. The sound of the running water gave Vanessa the urge to go to the bathroom. She closed the door.

Meanwhile, Mrs. Onero and Brandon were sitting in the kitchen eating their breakfast. Mrs. Onero told Brandon, "I don't know why Vanessa has been so tired lately. Maybe she has just been working really hard on her Florida report."

"Yeah. I'm sure that's it Mom. Could I please have some more orange juice?"

"Sure Brandon. While I get your orange juice, would you mind getting Vanessa out of bed? I didn't hear her get up."

"No problem Mom." Brandon got up from the table and went into Vanessa's room. He had a sure way to wake her up. He put his arms overhead and jumped on Vanessa's bed face down. To his surprise, he just bounced right back up. There was no Vanessa underneath the covers. Brandon got up and walked out of her room. He looked in the living room. No Vanessa. He looked in his parents' room. No Vanessa. He walked through the kitchen and into his room. Yet still, no Vanessa. "Ma, Vanessa is not in her room. I can't seem to find her."

"Did you check the bathroom?" Mrs. Onero asked. Brandon walked to the bathroom and knocked on the door. There was no reply. Brandon knocked on the door again, this time a little harder and asked, "Vanessa, are you in there?" Still, there was no reply. Brandon decided to ajar the door just a little and peek his head in. When Brandon opened the door, he saw Vanessa, but she certainly didn't see him. Brandon ran to his room to get his camera. Mrs. Onero looked at her son in wonder as he ran through the kitchen. Brandon got his camera and ran back to the bath-room. He motioned to his mom to keep quiet. Brandon opened the door and took a picture of Vanessa.

Mrs. Onero was curious to see what was going on. She couldn't help but let out a giggle when she witnessed her daughter sound asleep on the toilet! Mrs. Onero closed the door and pushed Brandon back into the kitchen. "Go finish eating. I will take care of this."

Mrs. Onero knocked on the bathroom door, "Vanessa, are you okay in there?" Vanessa did not reply. Mrs. Onero knocked on the door again, and then she opened it. Mrs. Onero put her hand on Vanessa's shoulder, gently shook her and said, "Wake up Vanessa."

Vanessa jerked when she heard her name. She looked confused when she opened her eyes. "Where am I?" she asked.

"Honey, you fell asleep on the toilet!"

Vanessa finally realized what had happened. In a flash, she leaped off the throne and washed her hands. Mrs. Onero could see that Vanessa felt embarrassed. She didn't say a word.

Vanessa went into the kitchen to eat breakfast. Her brother looked at her, laughed and said, "I never knew the throne was made for sleeping. I'll have to try it sometime." Mrs. Onero gave Brandon a stare that said his comment was inappropriate.

Mrs. Onero pulled Vanessa's hair away from her face and asked, "Are you all prepared for your report today?"

Vanessa's demeanor changed in an instant when she heard the word report. "I guess so."

Vanessa's mom patted her on the back. "I know you will do great!"

****

97

The next thing Vanessa knew, Mrs. Techlander called her to the front of the room. Vanessa held onto the edge of her desk and swallowed hard. The lump in her throat was so big, she felt like she had just swallowed a whole apple. Vanessa slowly got up from her desk and went to the front of the room. Her heart started pounding faster when she saw all of her classmates' eyes on her. She hoped that the apple of a lump wasn't going to come up the wrong way. Mrs. Techlander broke the silence, "You may begin Vanessa."

Vanessa started her report by saying, "My report is all about Florida." Vanessa was looking at Mrs. Techlander and wondered if she should go through with telling the truth. There was silence. Mrs. Techlander pulled off her glasses, looked at Vanessa and said, "Miss Onero, we are waiting. If you do not have anything to share with us, sit down and stop wasting our time."

"Oooh, Mrs. Techlander, I have something to share with you and the class indeed. I need the help of the Internet."

"That is not a problem. I just hope that what you are doing is relevant," Mrs. Techlander told Vanessa.

Vanessa ran to the classroom computer and typed: WWW.WINGS. Vanessa waited a moment, only for the screen to display: SITE NOT FOUND. Vanessa quickly clicked the mouse several times and then did the same to the enter key. She was hoping to activate the site. Nothing happened. Vanessa took a deep

98

breath and told herself not to panic. Vanessa tried typing the address again. Nothing happened. Vanessa turned around and saw Mrs. Techlander glaring over her shoulder. Suddenly, Vanessa had an idea. She bounced away from the computer and flipped the classroom lights off. Then she proceeded to tell all of her classmates that they all had to wish they were at Disney World. Mrs. Techlander was still glaring at Vanessa, but didn't say anything to her. Vanessa went back to the computer and typed in WWW.WINGS. Once again, the screen displayed: SITE NOT FOUND.

Mrs. Techlander marched over to the lights, flicked them on and demanded, "Vanessa Onero, get away from that computer and on with your report right this instance!"

Without hesitation, Vanessa did as she was told. She went to the front of the class and said, "I bet you are all wondering what I'm trying to do here. You see, I wanted to make my report ultra exciting for you. I did not want to come up here and bore you with a bunch of facts about Florida. I wanted to share an amazing experience I had with you." Vanessa could see that she had everyone's attention, including Mrs. Techlander's, so she kept on talking. "Instead of just talking about Florida, I wanted to take you there. We can learn so much from actually being somewhere. I discovered a web site that will actually take you any-where you *really* want to go." Vanessa turned around and wrote WWW.WINGS on the chalkboard. "This web site took me to Florida beaches and Disney World in the past two days. I wanted you too, to experience this."

Mrs. Techlander interrupted Vanessa, "I think we have heard enough Vanessa. Go back to your seat." Vanessa did not want to obey Mrs. Techlander's order. She wanted to finish her story. "With all your respect Mrs. Techlander, please allow me a few more minutes to explain."

"Fine Vanessa. You have two minutes."

Vanessa told the class as much as she possibly could in the two minutes she was allowed. Most of her classmates did not seem to believe her, however. Mrs. Techlander made Vanessa take her seat and told her that she would talk to her after school. Vanessa couldn't believe what had just happened. For once, she was trying to tell the whole truth, and no one believed her!

When the afternoon was over, it was time for Vanessa to chat with Mrs. Techlander. Mrs. Techlander first told Vanessa, "I'm glad to see that you have quite an imagination young lady, but you have not completed your task."

"But Mrs. Techlander, what I tried to do in class really happened. Twice! I did it at home and it really worked."

"Whether your little wings worked or not is really besides the point Vanessa. I don't remember giving you an assignment that involved finding "wings." I will be calling your parents to tell them what happened today. You still owe me a ten-page report. We will discuss the due date tomorrow."

Vanessa felt as if Mrs. Techlander just hit her over the head with a baseball bat. She decided that she wasn't going to say another word. She just went to her locker, put her bulky winter attire on and went home.

Something to think about......

Vanessa felt as if Mrs. Techlander just hit her over the head with a baseball bat. Draw a picture of what this would look like. Then write words all around the picture to express how Vanessa must have felt in this situation with Mrs. Techlander.

Chapter 15
The Bribe

That night, Vanessa's parents weren't too pleased after they talked with Mrs. Techlander.

"Young lady, you have a lot of explaining to do!" Mr. Onero yelled. "I want you to go to your room and think about what you have done. Your mother and I will come and talk to you in just a few minutes." Vanessa raged to her room and closed the door. She jumped on her bed and began pounding her fists as fast as a heavyweight champion. *What am I going to do? If I tell my parents the truth, they won't believe me either. I'm doomed!* Vanessa stood on her bed and began jumping out her frustration. As she was jumping, she noticed a white envelope on her desk. It had her name printed on it in big bold letters. *Hmm. I wonder what that could be?* Vanessa jumped off her bed, eager to see what was inside the envelope. She opened the envelope, yanked out a piece of paper and a picture fell to the floor. Vanessa opened up the paper. It read:

VANESSA,

I HEARD WHAT HAPPENED AT SCHOOL TODAY. MRS. TECHLANDER TOLD MOM AND DAD THAT YOU TRIED THAT WINGS THING ON OUR HOME COMPUTER! YOU BETTER NOT TELL MOM AND DAD HOW YOU GOT THE PASSWORD. IF YOU

DO—I WILL MAKE SEVERAL COPIES OF THIS
PICTURE OF YOU AND I WILL GIVE ONE TO
EVERYONE AT YOUR SCHOOL!

Vanessa bent down to pick up the picture. Sure
enough, it was a picture of her sleeping on the toilet.
She wondered how Brandon got the film developed so
quickly. *Now what am I going to do? I can't let everyone at school see this picture. They already think I'm
crazy because of what I did in class today.* Just then,
Vanessa heard a knock at her door. "Just a minute
please." Vanessa stuffed the letter and picture into the
envelope, threw it into her closet, and then opened the
door to let her parents in.

"Well Vanessa, what do you have to say for
yourself?" Mr. Onero asked.

"Well you see Dad, I had a really wonderful experience and I just wanted to share it with my class,
but no one believed me."

"Vanessa, I don't quite understand what is going
on here, but you need to answer some questions for
us," Mr. Onero said as he sat Vanessa down on her
bed. "Vanessa, what exactly is WWW.WINGS?

"Well Dad, it's kind of hard to believe, but it is a
web site that will physically take you anywhere you
want to go. If you really believe, it gives you wings!"

Mr. and Mrs. Onero looked at Vanessa in awe
and Mrs. Onero said, "Where did you ever get an out-
rageous idea like that?"

"Well you see Mom, I just made it up. I was
bored with the rest of the web sites I was using, so I
made up my own!"

104

"Okay Vanessa, let me ask you another question. Where and when were you able to try out this site that you miraculously came up with?" Mr. Onero asked with an attitude.

Vanessa crossed her fingers behind her back and took a moment before she answered her father. "Well Dad, I have a confession to make. I've been sneaking into your office to use your computer." Mr. Onero's eyebrows came closer together, his nostrils flared and his lips pressed close together. For a moment, Vanessa thought she saw steam coming out of his ears! Mr. Onero opened up his mouth to say something, but Vanessa stopped him. "Before you say anything, I'd like to tell you that I know what I did was wrong. It was disrespectful and I promise, I will never let it happen again."

Mr. Onero was more disappointed than he was upset with his daughter. "But Vanessa, you knew that was part of your punishment. How could you disobey me like that? AND, how in the world did you get a hold of the password?"

Vanessa wanted to so badly rat on her brother. After all, he did have a speeding ticket her parents did not know about. On the other hand, she envisioned what school would be like if everyone saw the picture of her sleeping on the toilet. She had to think of something, quick! "Well Dad, I guess you could say that I kind of discovered the password in the same way I discovered WWW.WINGS." Vanessa's parents looked at her in a way that showed they knew she was bluffing.

"Well Vanessa, it really doesn't matter because I have changed my password, and no one in this house will be allowed to use it. After you show your mother and I some respect, I will consider giving it to you. Until then however, you are grounded until your birthday."

"My birthday? That's so unfair! My birthday is not until May! You can't do this to me!" Vanessa instantly began to cry.

"Oh yes we can," Vanessa's mother replied. "Vanessa, we've been nothing but fair to you. You need to start showing some respect and responsibility around here!"

Vanessa was sobbing. "Why...don't...you...believe...me? I am...telling...the...truth. I swear I am!"

Mrs. Onero hugged her daughter and said, "Lay down and get some rest. I will come and get you when dinner is ready." Vanessa's parents left her room and closed the door.

Vanessa couldn't believe what had just happened. For once in her life, she tried to tell the truth, but no one, not even her own parents believed her. And Brandon, she could just kill him! How dare he take a picture of her in such a private place! She'll get him back somehow. She knew she would.

Vanessa laid down on her bed and thought about her horrible day. She realized that Mrs. Techlander still expected her to finish the ten-page report. *I'll deal with her tomorrow,* she thought. Vanessa really didn't care about her Florida report, she just wished she could take another adventure on WWW.WINGS. She knew that was next to impossible because her father changed the password. Vanessa was unhappy with her day's turnout. She did feel content about one thing, however. She was happy to know that she took an adventure that no one else ever had taken before. She was the founder of WWW.WINGS. The adventures she had taken in the past two days, she will remember for as long as she lives.

Something to think about......

Do you think that Vanessa's parents believed that she figured out the password on her own? Why or why not?

Was Brandon's bribe an ethical thing to do?

Chapter 16
The New Project

The next morning, Vanessa woke up before her alarm clock. To her mother's surprise, she was showered and dressed just in time for breakfast. "Well Nessa, it's a pleasure to see you have yourself together this morning."

Vanessa gave her mom a hug and said, "Thanks for cooking breakfast for me Mom. You are the best!" Mrs. Onero gave her daughter a strange look as she sat down to eat. "Vanessa, honey," Mrs. Onero said.

"Yeah Mom?"

"I don't mean to burst your bubble this morning, but are you aware that is snowed again last night?"

"Eh, it's only cold, white stuff that likes to hang out here in the winter."

Mrs. Onero looked at Vanessa in wonder. She had no idea what had gotten into her little girl. She hoped that she wasn't up to any trouble. Mrs. Onero didn't say another word.

Once Vanessa reached school, she had a conference with Mrs. Techlander before science started. "Miss Onero, you know that you still have to complete your ten-page typed report. How much time do you think you need to complete it?"

Vanessa decided that she wasn't going to let Mrs. Techlander get under her skin. She was too con-

tent with herself. Vanessa thought for a moment before she answered Mrs. Techlander's question. *Well,
I'm grounded until my birthday. I suppose I could de-
vote some time to this project.* "How about I have it for
you in one week?"

Mrs. Techlander lowered her glasses down to the
tip of her nose and said, "One week? That will be fine,
no later. If you choose to be late again, your report
card grade for the quarter will be lowered. Do you understand Vanessa?" Vanessa shook her head up and
down. "Good. Now take your seat, please."

Mrs. Techlander went up to the front of the
room, sat on her stool and opened up her book. "Okay
class, I think we are ready to begin. I'd like you to
open up your science books to page 154, please." Everyone, even Vanessa, went into their desks, took out
their books and found page 154, just as Mrs. Techlander had asked them to. When Vanessa saw what
was on page 154, she suddenly got very excited.

"Class, I'd like you to observe this picture and
tell me what your thoughts are."

All of the students studied the picture, some
quite intensely. Some students turned their books upside down, hoping for a better angle. Vanessa knew
that she was looking at a picture of the solar system.
*Wow, I hope we can learn some neat stuff about outer
space.* Mrs. Techlander went around the room dis-
cussing the picture with the students. After she did
that, she went back up to the front of the room, sat on
the stool, and read to the class the first paragraph on
page 155. *Oh no. Not this again. Can't she think of
anything more interesting than to just read to us about*
110

the topic? As Vanessa began to flip through the pictures of the solar system, she started to daydream. Before she got too involved however, she stopped herself. She didn't want Mrs. Techlander to think that she wasn't paying attention. That was the last thing she needed. Vanessa forced herself to stay focused. She was never so bored in her entire life. If the science readings had lasted any longer, Vanessa would've jumped right out of her skin.

During recess that day, many of Vanessa's classmates ridiculed her about what happened in class the day before. "So Vanessa, how are your wings doing?" asked Robbie.

"Yeah Vanessa, I want you to close your eyes right now and really, really, really, wish you were at Disney World," said Paul.

"You better be careful Vanessa, I am the founder of WWW.AIRPLANE, I might crash into you during flight!" said another kid.

Vanessa simply walked away from all the comments. She knew that she had the same friends as she did from the day before. She skipped along to play with Erin and the other girls. Instead of being upset by the boys' comments, she did not care one bit. She was perfectly content knowing that she really did take those adventures. She was the founder of WWW.WINGS. And somehow, Vanessa knew that it was not over. She knew that she would be taking another adventure. "Hey Vanessa," called out one of the girls, "do you want to build a snowman with us?"

Vanessa hurried over so she could get in on the fun. As the girls were playing, one of them brought up

111

the solar system. "What kind of project do you think Mrs. Techlander will make us do on the solar system?"

Another girl looked at Vanessa and said, "You know what would be really cool?"

"What?" they all asked in harmony.

"I think it would be really cool if we could actually travel in space. You know, visit the other planets and stuff."

"Yeah, that would be awesome," said Vanessa. "But let's face it, you know Mrs. Techlander is going to give us some lame project."

"Well, I just think it would be really cool if we could get there somehow," Erin said as she looked at Vanessa.

"Vanessa, do you think that WWW.WINGS would be able to get us there?"

Vanessa couldn't believe that someone else believed that WWW.WINGS actually existed. "Well, I'm not sure. The key to getting to where you want to go with WWW.WINGS is really believing in the magic. If you don't believe, it won't work. That is why it didn't work in class yesterday.

Just then Mrs. Techlander blew the whistle for everyone to go inside. All of the kids began racing to get in line. Vanessa's mind was racing with ideas. Vanessa was fascinated by the solar system and wished she could know more about it. She wondered how far away those places really were. What exactly goes on there? Are there animals, people and schools? Or is it like they show in the movies, places that have strange one-eyed creatures? Vanessa didn't know the answers to any of these questions, but she was determined to find out. As Vanessa went back into the building, she was overwhelmed with joy. She couldn't wait to find out what life was like on Mars.

Something to think about......

What is your opinion?
After reading, do you think that Vanessa has SAD (seasonal affective disorder), or does she just have the "winter blues?"

"If you really believe, anything is possible." Vanessa had computer magic because she "really believed." How do you think this could relate to your own life? If you "really believe" in yourself, you could accomplish your goals. What are your goals for yourself?

My goal for this year:

My goal in five years:

My goal for the future:

Remember, if you "really believe" in yourself, and are willing to work hard, you could accomplish anything you want to. Good Luck!

About the Author

M. A. Kokos Lambrou believes that you should find a balance between exercising your mind and your body. She teaches elementary school academics and also teaches fitness classes for adults and children. M.A. Kokos Lambrou was named after both her grandmothers. "M" is for Maria and "A" is for Alexandra. She resides in Naperville, Illinois with her husband. Visit her website at www.makokoslambrou.com

My Favorite Internet sites!